August 21, 1905
To Whom It May Concern,
    I am sorry that I have to write this in a secret code. But I must do so in case Emily or John finds this letter. What I have hidden is much too valuable for them.
    I got the idea for the hiding place after our unfortunate flood. Use the simple instructions on the next page and the map. You will not have any difficulty finding it.

There *was* a treasure. And if, after more than eighty-five years, nobody had found the map, then maybe nobody had found the treasure, either!

THE GREAT TREASURE HUNT

Suzanne Allen

Illustrated by Cornelius Van Wright

SPLASH™

A BERKLEY / SPLASH BOOK

SCRAMBLED EGGS #4, THE GREAT TREASURE HUNT,
is an original publication of The Berkley Publishing Group.
This work has never appeared before in book form.

A Berkley Book/published by arrangement with General
Licensing Company, Inc.

PRINTING HISTORY
Berkley edition/November 1990

ISBN: 0-425-12477-0
RL: 3.5

A BERKLEY BOOK® TM 757,375
Berkley Books are published by
The Berkley Publishing Group,
200 Madison Avenue, New York, New York 10016.
The name "BERKLEY" and the "B" logo are trademarks
belonging to Berkley Publishing Corporation.

PRINTED IN THE UNITED STATES OF AMERICA

10 9 8 7 6 5 4 3 2 1

Chapter One

The big old house that now belonged to the Turner family had air vents at the very top, under each peak of the roof. They helped to keep the rafters dry and cool in hot weather. The vents looked like several dark slits in the peeling paint.

But, sometimes, in late afternoon when the sun was just right, it was possible to see a faint pale patch inside those slits. It might have been a ghostly white face, trapped forever high in the rafters.

The pale patch was, in fact, a letter. It had been written more than eighty-five years ago. The letter had never been delivered.

Late one Saturday afternoon, the sun was just right, and a ghost-white face looked down on the backyard at two young girls. The pair did not look up. The only faces they saw, or even imagined, were each other's. The two nine-year-old girls were much too busy arguing to see anything.

Nattata, nattata, nattata went Beryllium Turner and her stepsister Terri. They were getting on the nerves of the Turner family. That meant they were annoying a lot of people.

When Nicholas Turner married Lily Sterling, he brought his children to live in the rambling old Sterling house in San Diego. The house had belonged to the Sterling family for generations. Now Turners lived there, too. In fact, they were all Turners now, since the Sterlings had changed their name.

Together, the Turners and the Sterlings added up to a large family. Or two small volleyball teams.

That Saturday afternoon, the Turners were busy being two small volleyball teams. An old badminton net was strung on two poles at the back of the yard.

The True Turner Terrifics were playing the Former Sterling Fantastics. The family did not always divide up this way for volleyball. But they often did, because these two teams were quite evenly matched.

It was easy to tell a member of Former Sterling Fantastics. They all wore sloppy clothing and were covered in grass stains.

The Former Sterlings were led by Mrs. Turner. She had played volleyball at college. Because of this, the Former Sterlings met in huddles to make plans. They *sounded* like a smooth, professional volleyball team.

"Right, I'll feed the ball to Vanessa. She sets it up. Isabella, you dummy a shot. Then Tristan will spike it," whispered Mrs. Turner. They all clapped their hands, jumped out of the huddle.

A moment later, the ball came to Mrs. Turner. Expertly, she served it into the air. It disappeared in the afternoon sun. Sixteen-year-old Vanessa squinted and ducked. The ball hit her on the forehead anyway.

Twelve-year-old Izzy was meant to fake a shot. She swung wildly and hit the ball by mistake. Her fist carried on swinging. She spiked fourteen-year-old Tristan in the stomach.

"Izzy! You dummy!" gasped Tristan. He staggered backward and fell over Bart, their huge Newfoundland dog. Meanwhile, the ball bounced off Berry's ankles. She was too busy arguing with her stepsister to notice it.

That was the end of another fantastic play by the Former Sterling Fantastics.

The True Turner Terrifics were a completely different kind of volleyball team. They were led by Dorothea, their Australian housekeeper. She was not a true Turner at all. But she was necessary to make the teams even.

Dorothea was athletic and strong. "Come on! Let's have it!" she shouted as she dove for ball after ball.

Unfortunately, Dorothea had not played volleyball in school. Half the time, instead of hitting the ball up into the air, she made a great diving catch.

"Howzat?" she shouted as she caught the ball again. She lay on her stomach, holding it up for all to see.

The True Turner Terrifics scolded her. "This isn't cricket, Dorothea!"

"This isn't Australian football!"

Thanks to Dorothea, the True Turner Terrifics didn't sound smooth and professional. They sounded wild and enthusiastic. But, except for Dorothea, they all played very carefully. None of them wanted to wrinkle the neat white tennis outfits they all wore.

"It's yours, Paul!" called Mr. Turner as the ball flew over the net toward the True Turners.

Fifteen-year-old Paul barely leaned toward the ball. "It's closer to you, Melissa!" he called.

"No way!" sniffed thirteen-year-old Melissa. She struck a stylish pose as the ball dropped beside her. Melissa liked to imagine herself modeling sportswear.

The ball bounced in front of Mr. Turner. "I've got it!" he cried, much to everybody's surprise. Mr. Turner gave the ball a gentle patty-cake push. Everyone groaned.

"For goodness sake, Dad! Once it's hit the ground, it's *dead!*" scolded Paul. Mr. Turner was absolutely hopeless at volleyball.

That was the end of another terrific play by the True Turner Terrifics.

Meanwhile, an argument was raging across the net. "Just because you're older than me doesn't mean you know *everything!*" said Terri.

"Yeah? All right then, if you're so smart, tell me this. How many, um . . . do we have in our house?" said Berry.

"How many *what?*" said Terri.

"Let me think. I know. Barbecues!" said Berry.

"Who cares?" said Mr. Turner.

"Be quiet and play, you two," said Mrs. Turner. But it was no use.

"I thought so! She doesn't know!" said Berry. "That's just one *more* thing she doesn't know about our house!"

5

"Please, can't we gag them both?" moaned Vanessa.

Terri thought carefully. She had only lived in the house for months, not years. But already she knew a lot about it. On her very first day there, Terri had searched the house. She discovered it was absolutely chock-full of junk.

Terri had grown up in a super-tidy condominium townhouse. She thought all the Sterling junk was gross. But fascinating, too!

Somewhere in all the clutter she had hoped to find a bedroom of her own. No such luck, though. Terri was still stuck sharing with her stepsister.

Berry was three days older than Terri and three times more annoying than the whole rest of the family put together.

"Well?" said Berry, hands on her hips.

"One," said Terri, pointing to the big gas barbecue on the patio beside the back door.

"One," counted Berry.

"And there's an old one in the garage."

"Two," said Berry.

"*And* down in the basement, one of the cat's litter boxes is the bottom of a barbecue," said Terri triumphantly. "That's three. Three barbecues is the answer. So there!"

"Wrong!" said Berry smugly.

Looking very important, she walked toward the back door. Terri followed her. Everyone else stood about and sighed. They'd rather play volleyball than listen to an argument.

Berry stopped beside the three steps up to the back door. She crouched down and pointed to a wooden lattice covered in peeling green paint that screened off the gap under the steps.

"This comes out. Didn't you know *that?*" said Berry. She sounded as if it was the single most important thing in the world to know.

Berry tugged at the lattice. Thick grass had grown up around it, but finally it came free. Under the steps was a small pile of bricks, a collection of green plastic flower pots, and a large round shape completely brown with rust.

"That's a barbecue, too," said Berry. She rapped the rusty circle with her knuckles. "See?"

"It's a piece of junk, like everything else around here," Terri said, rather too loudly.

"Terri!" called her father sharply.

"Sorry," muttered Terri, glancing back at her stepmother across the yard.

"I'm sorry, too," called Mrs. Turner cheerfully. "But the Sterling family and junk have always seemed to go together, like peanut butter and jelly."

"You'll *never* know as much about this house as me!" crowed Berry. Terri scowled and looked at the ground.

"Personally, I've never heard such a stupid, useless argument in my life," said Vanessa.

Chapter Two

Mrs. Turner and Vanessa were washing the supper dishes. Out in the dining room, they could hear Berry and Terri. The youngest Turners had driven the whole family out of the dining room. It was the same old argument.

"What is it this time? How many windows? How many washcloths?" said Mrs. Turner to Vanessa.

"I'm beginning to think they'll never stop," said Vanessa.

"Maybe if Terri finally knew something that Berry didn't," said Mrs. Turner.

"Maybe," said Vanessa. "But I think it would have to be a pretty big something in order to stop the argument for good."

"Hmm," said Mrs. Turner. She and her eldest daughter stood at the sink, looking thoughtful.

That night, Terri had a dream. It was quite remarkable. Even as she was having the dream, Terri was saying to herself, Boy! I've never noticed the smell of perfume in a dream before! It was a beautiful smell.

Terri dreamed that she was watching herself sleep. Suddenly she realized she was not alone in the bedroom. A strange, ghostly figure was drifting toward her bed. Like a mist, it folded around the head of her sleeping body. Am I there, or here? wondered Terri as she lay and watched.

She must have been in both places, because a whisper curled like frost around her ear. "Look at the top floor, Terri," said the figure. "Look *closely* at the top floor."

Now, the figure was standing beside her, its hand outstretched, inviting. Terri took the hand and floated out, across the landing, and up the stairs toward the top floor.

Then, halfway up the stairs Terri suddenly felt frightened. I'm holding hands with a ghost! she thought, squeezing her eyes shut in terror.

Terri awoke in her bed. She was shivering, even though it was a warm night. There was nobody in the room with her, nobody but Berry, sound asleep in the next bed. And yet the dream had seemed so real!

* * *

In the morning Terri had forgotten all about her nighttime visitor.

Sunday was a slow day in the Turner house. Berry and Terri planned to do nothing much, but in several interesting ways. They hadn't counted on Mr. Turner, who arrived last to breakfast and brought a small cloud of gloom with him.

Mr. Turner took a sip or two of coffee, then said cheerfully, "By the way, how's that school history project of yours coming along?" He was looking right at Berry and Terri.

Berry and Terri glanced at each other nervously. The project was due in a week, and so far they hadn't done a thing about it.

That was normal for last-minute Berry. But this time, Terri was dragging her heels, too. She hated history more than any other subject. It was so dull!

Mr. Turner read his answer in their faces. "Well, of course, I don't want to spoil your Sunday, but I think you should listen to me for a moment," said Mr. Turner.

Uh-oh! He's going to make a speech! thought everybody around the table. When Mr. Turner started talking at mealtimes, hot drinks froze over, and food went moldy.

12

One by one, almost everybody crept away. Berry and Terri stayed. They were stuck.

Mercifully, the speech was quite short. It was about schoolwork getting more complicated as grades got higher. It was about the disasters that happened when complicated work was left until the last minute.

Like all of Mr. Turner's speeches, it was full of little sayings. He spoke them so seriously! Just as if he'd made them up only a moment before.

"And the moral is this," he said at last, "when you make your own bed, you must lie in it." He looked seriously from face to face.

"Gosh, thanks for reminding us, Dad! We haven't made our beds!" said quick-thinking Terri, jumping to her feet. Berry followed her out of the room.

Free at last, the two girls ran upstairs giggling and whispering to each other.

"A rolling stone gathers no moss," said Berry.

"A stitch in time saves nine," said Terri.

But even though they were making fun of Mr. Turner, they both knew in their hearts that Sunday would not be a lazy play day after all. It was going to be a dull day buried in history books.

And then, Mr. Turner accidentally changed everything. He stepped out into the hallway and heard the two girls whispering on the stairs.

"Whisper, whisper, whisper!" he called after them. "That better be history you're whispering in each other's ears!"

Berry was surprised to see her stepsister stop on the landing and stare off into space, an odd expression on her face. Her father's words had reminded Terri of her strange dream.

Last night, some words had been whispered into her ear. It had all been a dream, surely! Or had someone, or even—shudder—something, visited her in the middle of the night?

What on earth were the words? Somehow, Terri felt they were important. Gradually, a picture formed in her mind. It was the roof of the Sterling house. So what about it?

Terri went downstairs, through the front door, and out to the sidewalk. Holding up her hand to block the light of the sunny sky, she stared back at the old Sterling house.

"Look at the top floor, look closely at the top floor," the figure in her dream had said. Terri remembered the words as clearly as if she had been awake. What was she meant to see?

There were two bedrooms on the top floor. Their windows faced the front. Terri studied those windows now. One was in Paul's room. The other in Tristan's. Big deal.

Terri walked along the sidewalk for a little way. Now she could see the roof of the house stretching toward the backyard.

Was there anything special about the roof? Not really. It began above the two windows in the front, and ran straight back. For some reason, she continued to stare at it.

After a while, a thought began to form in Terri's mind. Wasn't it strange that there were *five* bedrooms and a bathroom on the second floor of the house. But, there were only two bedrooms and a large linen closet on the top floor above it.

And those two top-floor rooms were not very big. Certainly not big enough to take up the whole top floor. What exactly *was* under the roof at the back of the house?

Suddenly Terri knew the answer. The house had an attic! And yet, how could that be? Nobody had ever breathed a word about it to her.

Terri forgot all about history projects. A minute later she was wandering from room to room on the second floor of the house staring at the ceiling.

15

Berry, reading on her bed, saw her come and go. What *was* Terri up to? Berry was curious. But she thought it might be better to avoid her stepsister today. Terri might start to nag her about that darned history project, and Berry really didn't feel much like doing homework on such a splendidly lazy day.

Terri was looking for a trapdoor leading from the second floor up to the third floor. She slipped into Izzy's room. There was no Izzy, and no trapdoor, either.

There was no trapdoor above the landing, in the bathroom, nor in her parents' room or closet. There was no trapdoor in Vanessa's room or Melissa's room.

That left only one place left to look. Terri went into her own bedroom with her eyes still glued to the ceiling. She nearly killed herself stumbling across a litter of junk on Berry's side of the room.

"What's the matter?" said Berry. "Have you got a nose bleed, or have—?" Berry was left with her mouth hanging open. Terri marched straight across the bedroom, went into their closet, and closed the door.

A moment later the door opened and Terri came out again. Frowning, she sat on her bed.

"Have you gone *crazy?*" said Berry. "What were you doing in the closet?"

Terri was not listening. She stood up suddenly and swept out of the room.

"Yes," Berry answered herself. "My serious step-twin has suddenly gone loony."

Chapter Three

Terri stood on the little top-floor landing, working her lips to help her think. She looked as though she were rinsing with mouthwash.

Since there was no attic door in any of the walls, there were only two answers left.

Maybe the attic was walled off. In that case, there was no way in, and nothing to find.

Or maybe there was a hidden door. If so, there was only once place it could be. Terri pulled open the door to the large linen closet. It was piled high on three sides with shelves of blankets, sheets, and pillowcases.

Terri pulled a stack of sheets from a shelf on her right. She reached in where they had been and felt along the wall. It felt just like a wall.

She removed a pile of blankets from the rear shelf and reached into the darkness beyond. This time the wall felt uneven. Hmm.

Terri stepped out of the closet, still carrying the stack of blankets. She knocked on one of the two bedroom doors.

"Come in!" Terri stepped into a true Turner room. It was neat as a pin. Her brother Paul was inside, studying for an exam.

"Paul, could I stack some blankets on your bed for a little while?" she said.

Paul frowned at his homework. "I'd rather you didn't," he said without looking up. "Take them down to your pigsty, why don't you?"

"Thanks," said Terri. She made a face at his back. Typical.

Next, she tried her stepbrother in the other bedroom. Tristan was lying on the bed, earphones on his head, tapping his feet to silent music. Why go downstairs to find a pigsty? thought Terri. Tristan's room was a truly disgusting mess.

"Tristan!" shouted Terri. Tristan lifted an earphone away from his head and grinned.

"Can I stack some blankets on your bed for a minute?" she said.

"If you can find the room, you're welcome to it," he said, and went back to his music.

In the end, Terri had blankets stacked all over Tristan's legs. He didn't seem to mind at all.

The wide back shelves of the closet were nothing but boards resting across the side shelves. One by one, Terri lifted them up, turned them sideways, and stood them on the floor.

Even before she was finished, she could see that the wall behind the shelves was not a wall at all. It was a narrow wooden door with a brass doorknob.

She smiled to herself as she removed the last board. Gotcha, Berry! she said to herself. But she hadn't *quite* got Berry yet. When Terri tried to open the door, it was locked.

Mrs. Turner was sitting in the old rocking chair on the front porch, reading. "What is it, Terri?" said Mrs. Turner, looking up.

"Um . . . did you know there was a door at the back of the linen closet?"

A shadow seemed to fall across Mrs. Turner's face. For a moment, she looked away.

Uh-oh! thought Terri. I've done something wrong. "Are you okay?" she said anxiously.

Mrs. Turner turned back and gave Terri a small smile. Then she stood and kissed her stepdaughter on the forehead.

"Yes, I'm all right, Terri," she said. "And I *do* know about the door. You were very clever to find it. Now, I suppose you'd like the key?"

Terri's heart leapt. "Yes, please," she said. A

moment later Terri was scampering up the stairs, a small brass key in her hands.

The Turner family took turns cooking Sunday lunch. Today was the worst Sunday of the month—the Sunday when it was Izzy and Melissa's turn to cook. They always made the same thing: hot dogs on the barbecue in the backyard.

"Lunchtime!" shouted Izzy. The whole family came running, but not because they were looking forward to lunch.

They ran because the Turner family still did not have enough chairs in the backyard to go around. Latecomers had to sit on the grass, or on the back steps.

Berry was one of the first to arrive. She looked suspiciously at the hot dogs on the large platter beside the barbecue.

Izzy and Melissa cooked hot dogs two ways, too much and not enough. There were hot-dogsicles. Barely warm on the outside, they were so cold inside that they snapped if you tried to bend them. The rest of the hot dogs were crisped to a crunch.

It took only a second for Berry to make up her mind. She ignored the hot dogs and filled her bun with relish and ketchup.

Last to arrive was Terri. One by one the family saw her. One by one they stopped eating and gaped in astonishment.

Terri was normally as neat and clean as all the true Turners. Now, for some reason, she was absolutely filthy! Her jeans and T-shirt were covered in gray-black stains. Only her hands and face were impeccably clean. (True Turners always washed before eating.)

"Whatever happened to you?" said her astonished father.

Terri just looked smug. She turned the dial at the side of the barbecue and restarted it. Then she did what several others had already done. Terri put a hot-dogsicle back on the grill and began to cook it properly.

"Really, wherever have you been, Terri?" said her brother Paul.

"Don't come near me!" said her sister Melissa.

"Did you accidentally rub against Berry?" wondered Vanessa. Terri refused to answer any questions until she had finished sizzling her hot dog.

Finally, when everybody was bursting with curiosity, Terri looked over at her stepsister and spoke. "Beryllium, if *you* know so much about this house, how many rooms are there on the top floor?" she said.

Berry looked at Terri oddly.

"Two, of course," she said.

"Wrong!" said Terri.

"Oh, all right! Five, then," said Berry. "If you want to count the two bedroom closets and the linen closet."

"Wrong again!" crowed Terri.

"Terri, I'm not *stupid,* you know," said Berry. "Although, maybe *you* are."

"Suppose I told you there are *three* rooms on the top floor?" said Terri.

"Suppose I told you that you're nuts?" said Berry.

"And that the third room is bigger than *every other room in the house!*"

Berry didn't answer. She just looked around at the family and spun her finger around her ear to let them all know that Terri had gone crazy.

"I'll show you," said Terri, standing and waving for Berry to follow.

Melissa and Paul were curious, too. "Can we come, Terri?" asked Melissa.

"You can *all* come," said Terri.

Except for Berry, the former Sterling kids all

hesitated. "Is this all right, Mom?" said Vanessa at last.

Mrs. Turner gave a small, sad smile. "It's about time, don't you think? You all go. Don't wait for me," she said.

About time for what? wondered Berry as she followed her stepsister. Mrs. Turner's words had made her uneasy. Was there something important about the house that she didn't know, after all?

The true Turners, including Mr. Turner, were right after Berry. The former Sterling kids crowded everybody from behind. They wanted to stick close to their youngest sister and watch that superior smile get wiped off her face.

"Here we are," said Terri as everyone crowded onto the landing of the top floor.

Berry snorted. "This is pathetic!" she said. "You can't say a hallway is a room, Terri! You *still* don't know anything about—"

Berry's voice failed as Terri swung open the door to the linen closet. Beyond it was another door, also open. And beyond that, lit by a string of dusty light bulbs, was a long attic, crisscrossed with rafters and filled to the brim with every kind of junk imaginable.

Berry was stunned. Berry was angry. Berry spluttered. "Why? How? But, but—!"

"Well!" It was Mr. Turner speaking. "I must say I'm surprised to see this attic myself." He pushed his way forward through the crowd and peered through the door of the linen closet. "Was it supposed to be some kind of secret?"

Everyone looked at Vanessa except Berry, who was staring speechless and bug-eyed through the linen closet door. She blinked her eyes, hoping what she saw before her would somehow vanish.

Meanwhile, Vanessa looked uncomfortable. "Well, it's not a *secret,*" she said finally. "But when our father died, Mom stored a lot of his old stuff in here. After that she didn't want to go in the attic, much. None of us did."

"Oh," said Mr. Turner, looking uncomfortable himself.

"And Tristan stuck up the shelves at the back of the closet, and they filled up, and . . . Well, anyway, I guess Mom's finally decided, well, that, well . . ."

Vanessa's voice was breaking now. "Excuse me," she said, and disappeared down the stairs to her room. Vanessa had grown very fond of her stepfather. But she still missed her real father the most of all the former Sterling kids, even after five years.

There was a very long, awkward silence. Mr. Turner stepped into the closet and poked his nose into the attic. He backed out in a hurry, dusting off his hands.

"No wonder you look so filthy, Terri!" he said.

He closed the closet door firmly and shooed everybody toward the stairs. "I'm afraid anybody who wants to explore the attic *must* clean it first," said Mr. Turner.

After what Vanessa had said, Terri did not think it right to crow about her great discovery. She couldn't resist a smug little smile, though, as she disappeared down the stairs.

Berry was the last to leave the landing. She stood staring angrily at the linen closet door, as if it were a friend who had betrayed her. "Why? Why didn't *I* know about the attic?" she wailed. It was totally humiliating.

Under the covers in her bed that night, she was still sulking as she wrote in her diary.

My dear true twin sister Annamarie,
    You have not seen me since we were separated at birth nine years ago. But, get ready!

I will be running away from home any day now.

I am outraged! All my brothers and sisters knew we had an attic in our house. But nobody told me! They say that five years ago I was too young to play in it, and might have been hurt. Isn't that dumb?

Anyway, our nosy almost step-triplet, Terri, found the attic and made me look like a fool!

Well, I was going to make homemade Christmas cards this year for everybody. Instead, I had a bonfire in the backyard after lunch and burned all the paper I planned to use for the cards. Can you blame me?

I will be on my way to live with you in Paris, France, just as soon as I've checked out all the old junk in the attic. It's awesome!

Love,
Beryllium

P.S. Terri says she dreamed that someone told her about the attic. But the way it happened, I think she was awake. I think she saw a ghost!

Chapter Four

The letter fluttered down across the dusty rays of daylight that shone through the vent high above in the rafters. Terri stood on tiptoes, her arms upstretched, and watched it fall. She had knocked it from its perch with the rag-covered broom she was using to collect cobwebs.

"What's that?" said Terri. She lowered the broom and peered at the floor. There was nothing in sight. Surely it hadn't been her imagination?

No, Berry had seen it, too. A moment later they found it. It was almost invisible—a small, dirty envelope that had landed dusty side up on a dusty floor. Terri picked it up and wiped it off carefully.

The envelope was sealed, but not stamped. A single line of faded handwriting stretched neatly across one side: *"To Whom it May Concern."* The two girls looked at each other. Did it concern them?

It certainly did.

"Do you suppose it was hidden?" said Terri.

They both gazed up at the sharp sunlight streaming through the ventilation slots.

"You couldn't just leave it accidentally. Not way up there," said Berry.

"Open it," urged Terri.

But how could they open it? They had promised not to explore *any* of the junk in the attic until it was dust-free.

Berry instantly solved that problem. She carried the envelope out of the attic and down to their bedroom. "There. Now we can explore it, because it isn't in the attic," she said.

Terri thought Berry was a genius. "Go on! Open it!" she said.

"Here, you'd better do it," said Berry. It was a smart thing to say. Dogs, using only their teeth, could open letters more neatly than Berry.

Terri slit the envelope neatly and removed three small sheets of paper. They were all written in the same beautiful handwriting as the envelope.

At the top right-hand corner of the first page, there was a date: August 21, 1905.

"Gosh, that's old!" breathed Terri.

Below the date were the same words as on the envelope—*"To Whom it May Concern."*

The rest of the page was unreadable.

Berry snatched it from Terri and turned it this way and that. "It's some kind of code!" she whispered, her eyes wide.

Terri studied the writing over Berry's shoulder. Then she looked at the second page, still in her own hand.

"Not this page," she said. It was written in English, and was nothing but a short list of four items:

> gold
> three yards of pink satin ribbon
> my best dancing shoes
> a miniature painting of my mother

Terri passed the page to Berry. Berry read it and shrugged. It meant nothing to her.

The last page of the letter set Terri's heart pounding. It was a map.

"Let's see it," said Berry, trying to wrestle it from Terri.

"Be careful!" said Terri, holding it away from her. Berry studied it over Terri's shoulder.

Lines had carefully been ruled across the paper to guide the hand of the artist. The largest shape on the map was a square with a large chunk missing from the bottom right-hand corner.

In the center of the map, there was a circle. What really interested the two girls was what nestled right beside the circle. It was a large X! They looked at each other. In the bottom right-hand corner of the map were two faded initials: *A.S.*

Berry and Terri both knew exactly what they held in their hands. It *had* to be . . . a treasure map!

It was so exciting! For the longest time they sat on Berry's bed, saying "Gosh! Gosh! Gosh!" over and over again.

What was the treasure? Where was it buried? Who buried it? There were so many exciting questions! At first, it seemed there were no answers to any of them.

The girls snatched the pages of the letter back and forth, trying to make sense of each.

In the end, Terri said, "Let's each work on a different page. Otherwise, we'll tear the letter."

For the first time in weeks, there was no argument about who knew the house best. "You work on the map, Beryllium," said Terri. "If it's a map of any place around here, you're most likely to know it."

Terri herself tried to decipher the mysterious code on the first page of the letter.

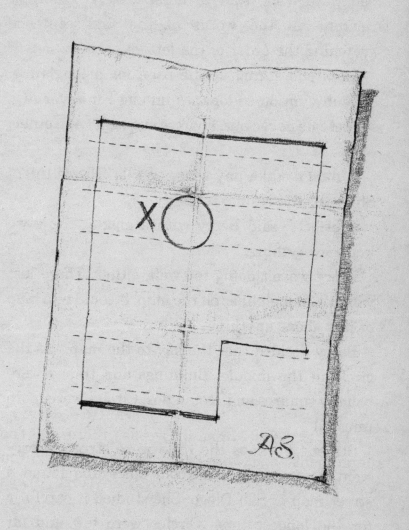

"Maybe the words are English, only written backward," she said to herself. Terri carefully rewrote all the words of the first sentence switching the order of the letters.

Then she stared at the page for a long time: "oneub yum on se lonapse im euq rop sever la y lonapse ne at rac atse rivircse euq ognet euq otneis oy."

It didn't make any sense at all. "How's this?" She read the results to Berry.

"Perfect," said Berry with a giggle. "Now we know everything."

Berry wasn't doing too well, either. There just weren't enough lines on the map. It could be a map of just about anything.

Berry decided that the key to the map was the circle in the middle. Buildings and things were usually squares and rectangles. Circles were more unusual.

Streets! Perhaps the lines were streets. Berry went down to the sun-room office and found a street map of San Diego. She studied it carefully for the longest time. Circles were few and far between. Berry soon realized that every circular road had other roads connected to it. And none had a square with a missing corner surrounding the circle.

Berry and Terri were still excited at bedtime that night. The more they looked at the word "gold" on the second page of the letter, the more certain they were that they had an old treasure map in their hands.

"S stands for Sterling, I'll bet," said Terri as she lay in the dark. She knew she didn't have to tell Berry what she was talking about. They were both thinking only of one thing: the map. "Berry?" Berry was silent. "Have you gone to sleep, Berry?"

When Berry finally spoke, it was in a low, spooky voice. "You know what I think, Terri? I think it *was* somebody Sterling who drew that map. Only I think they did something else, too. I think whoever it was knew that nobody had discovered the map. Not until now."

"That's silly," said Terri. "They're probably dead by now."

"Exactly! I think the ghost of A.S. wanted somebody to find that letter," whispered Berry.

"Stop speaking in a spooky voice!" said Terri crossly.

"The ghost wanted a Sterling to find it, and to

get the treasure," said Berry. "That's why it told you about the attic."

"Then why me?" said Terri. "I'm a Turner."

"So? Maybe it was looking for me and got confused in the dark."

"Oh, sure."

"Anyway, I can fix that," said Berry. She clicked on her bedside light.

"What are you doing?" asked Terri. Berry wrote "Berry Sterling" on one large sheet of paper, and "Terri Turner" on another. She placed them carefully on the correct beds.

"Just in case it comes back," said Berry, leaning over Terri to whisper hoarsely in her stepsister's ear.

Terri kicked the sign off her bed, angrily. "That's dumb, Berry!" she said.

Berry got back into her own bed and turned out the light. "I think we should turn over now and hope as hard as we can," whispered Berry.

"Hope for what?"

"Oh, please, ghost, come and tell us what the letter means. Please, please, ghost. Come back again," muttered Berry into her pillow.

"Shut up, Berry!" said Terri.

"One of us is going to feel a clammy hand on our

shoulder," said Berry. "And a cold breath in our ear. Be sure to listen carefully if it speaks to you, Terri. Terri?"

But Terri was on her way across the room to turn on the lights. Berry was filling her mind with memories of the first encounter with the ghost. Terri didn't want to repeat it.

"Hey! You'll scare the ghost away!" said Berry as the light clicked on.

"That's right," said Terri. "We'll just have to figure out the treasure map on our own."

For a little while they took turns getting out of bed and turning the light on, or off. At last, Berry grew bored and fell asleep. Terri turned the light on, and that's the way it stayed.

And sure enough, no ghost visited that night. Just in case, Terri kept her shoulders safely under the covers. No ghost was going to put its clammy hand on her when she wasn't looking!

Chapter Five

When Terri woke up the next morning, Berry was studying the code on the first page of the letter. She handed the page to Terri. "Read the first sentence aloud to me," she commanded.

Terri, still half asleep, did her best. "Bueno muy no es espanol mi que por reves al y espanol en carta esta escrivir que tengo que siento yo," she said.

"You know," said Berry, frowning, "it almost *sounds* like Spanish."

"Are you sure?"

" 'Que' is a Spanish word, I think," said Berry. "Only you were saying 'kuh' and I think it's supposed to be pronounced 'kay.' "

"I don't know," said Terri. "See this word—'no'? Well, 'no' is an English word. And this sure isn't English."

"All the same, it *might* be Spanish," insisted Berry.

"So okay, let's ask Vanessa, or Paul or—" began Terri.

Berry cut her off. "No!" she cried. "We *can't* let them know about this! We've got to find it first! They'll just hog all the fun, if they find out."

"All right. All right. So how are we going to find out if it's Spanish, then?" grumbled Terri.

They decided to risk showing one sentence to somebody. Terri copied it out neatly onto a blank sheet of paper.

They found Melissa in her room, getting dressed. Melissa was taking Spanish in school.

"Melissa, is this Spanish?" asked Terri.

Melissa frowned at the piece of paper. "What is this?" she said suspiciously.

"Nothing much," said Terri.

"We made it up," said Berry.

"You made it up and you don't know if it's *Spanish!*" said Melissa, looking at her young stepsister as though she had a screw loose.

"Well, we sort of copied some of it, too," said Terri, glancing at Berry. Let me do the talking, dimwit, her look said.

Melissa studied the paper. She frowned. Her frown grew.

"Well, it's *kind* of Spanish," she said at last. "Only it doesn't make much sense."

"What's it say?"

39

"It starts off . . . 'Good very not is Spanish,'" began Melissa. She looked up. "Maybe you copied it down wrong. Show me what you copied it from."

"Sorry, we can't," said Berry, snatching the piece of paper away from Melissa.

Melissa tried to grab it back, but missed. "What *is* it anyway?" she said. "Something you found in the attic? Dad said you couldn't start going through things till it was clean, remember?"

Melissa had to shout her last words, because Berry and Terri had scampered out of the room.

Even if they hadn't made perfect sense, the two girls were sure they were on the right track. The next step was to find the Spanish-English dictionary and take it to school with them.

Terri walked all the way to school with her nose buried in the dictionary. Berry had to guide Terri to keep her from bumping into things.

That day in school both Berry and Terri got into trouble with Mr. Marks, their class teacher, for "fooling around under your desk" and not paying attention. It was a small price to pay.

By the time they walked home that afternoon, they had translated the entire first page. *And* they knew why it hadn't made sense, at first. That's because every sentence was written backward.

Most important of all, they knew that their wildest hopes had been answered. The letter explained quite clearly that the map really *was* a treasure map.

August 21, 1905.
To Whom it May Concern.

I am sorry that I have to write this in Spanish, and backward, because my Spanish is not very good. But I must do so in case Emily or John finds this letter. What I have hidden is much too valuable for them.

I got the idea for the hiding place after our unfortunate flood. Use the simple instructions on the next page and the map. You will not have any difficulty finding it.

There *was* a treasure. And if, after more than eighty-five years, nobody had found the map, then maybe nobody had found the treasure, either!

Suddenly the list of four items on the second page became all-important. These were "simple instructions." The clues that were meant to clearly explain the map. That's what the letter said.

gold

three yards of pink satin ribbon

my best dancing shoes

a miniature painting of my mother

They were too excited to sit, so they paced. They wandered together around and around the backyard with the second page of the letter held in front of them. What could the words mean?

Try as they might they couldn't think of *anything*. Except "gold." They knew what THAT meant. It had to be the treasure! But the rest of the words . . .

"Three yards of satin ribbon?" said Terri. "Maybe we're supposed to use that to measure something with."

"Measure what?" said Berry with a sigh.

"Maybe from some pair of dancing shoes that are lying somewhere in the house?" suggested Terri.

"Well, if they were lying around in 1905, you can bet they're not in the same place today," said Berry.

"Yeah? I know how fast the Sterlings put stuff

away. They *might* still be in the same place," said Terri.

Berry scowled at her.

"So maybe it's a map of a shoe closet. Are any closets that shape?" said Terri.

"How can anyone bury treasure in a closet?" said Berry.

"You could in ours," Terri said. "There's so much junk in it." She was still trying to get Berry to help neaten it up.

"Listen, if you're going to keep on making nasty remarks—" said Berry angrily.

"Sorry, sorry," said Terri. They walked on for a little while in silence.

At last, Berry said, "I think we should try to find out who John and Emily and A.S. really were."

"Let's ask your mom," said Terri. "After all, we don't have to say anything about the map. Or the letter."

Chapter Six

Berry and Terri did their best to corner their mother alone before suppertime. She was cooking that evening, though. Every time Berry and Terri went into the kitchen, somebody else wandered in, too.

"Ask her during dinner," said Terri. "Nobody will know why we're asking, anyway."

Berry waited through supper until she thought the moment was right. Then she spoke. "Mom, when we were cleaning out the attic we saw some initials," she said.

"And a date," added Terri.

"Any idea who it might be?" said Berry.

"Not until you tell me what the initials are," said Mrs. Turner.

"A.S.," said Berry.

"1905," said Terri.

"What was it on?" said Tristan.

"None of your business," said Berry to her brother.

44

"They're up to something," announced Melissa to the whole table. Terri glared at her sister.

Meanwhile, Mrs. Turner had put down her knife and fork. She gazed up at the ceiling, her brow wrinkled. "1905," she said. "Well, this house was built in 1895. That means your great-great-grandfather, Joshua Sterling, was still living here with his second wife."

"What was her initial?" asked Berry.

"M. For Martha," said Mrs. Turner.

"So they would be J.S. and M.S.," said Terri.

Mrs. Turner nodded. "Joshua and Martha had two children, John and Emily. John was your father's grandfather, and your great-grandfather, Berry." Berry and Terri exchanged glances. John and Emily were the two names in the letter!

"That's another J.S. And an E.S.," said Berry. "So who was A.S.?"

"Mmm." Mrs. Turner was thinking. She knitted her brow. Then her face cleared. "Of course! I'm forgetting Andrew Sterling."

"A.S.!" said Terri triumphantly.

"That's right," said Mrs. Turner. "He was Joshua's son from his first marriage. He was much older than his stepbrother and stepsister and he more or less ran away from home. He got gold fever."

When Mrs. Turner spoke the word "gold," both Berry and Terri looked at each other. "What's gold fever?" said Berry.

"The urge to find gold becomes like a disease. There was the California Gold Rush, and later the Yukon Gold Rush. People rushed off to mine for gold and make their fortunes," said Mrs. Turner. "Andrew went north in the Yukon Gold Rush."

Berry and Terri looked at each other again. They thought they were being pretty cool about it, but everybody else around the table thought their eyeballs were going to fly out.

Suddenly everybody knew that Melissa was right. Berry and Terri *were* up to something!

"I didn't know you knew so much about Dad's family, Mom," said Vanessa.

Mrs. Turner got a wistful look on her face. "Oh, yes," she said. "Your father and I spent a great deal of time long ago researching both our family histories. And of course, I grew up around here, so I knew lots of Sterlings. Then when I came to live in this house, so rich with family history . . . well, it just seemed natural to know all these things."

Berry and Terri could barely conceal their impatience. This was all very interesting, they were both thinking, but let's get on with the hidden treasure!

"When was this Yukon Gold Rush thing, Mom?" said Berry.

Mrs. Turner shrugged.

"Somehow the year 1896 sticks in my mind," said Mr. Turner.

"But, if he left in 1896, then how would the date 1905 make any sense?" said Paul, serious as always.

Terri opened her mouth to tell her oldest brother to butt out.

Vanessa spoke first. "Maybe the two of them would like to tell us all a little more about where they saw this name and the date," she said.

"We wouldn't like to tell *you* anything, Vanessa," said Berry.

"Andrew did come back home, I believe," said Mrs. Turner. "To show off to his father, mainly. That's because he *did* make his fortune in the gold rush."

Once again, nobody in the family could miss the excited glances that Berry and Terri traded.

"It *could* have been 1905," continued Mrs. Turner. "After that, he went back to the Yukon."

47

"And then?" said Berry.

"And then nobody ever heard from him again," said Mrs. Turner. Berry and Terri looked at each other once more. They were both thinking exactly the same thought.

Andrew Sterling, who had made a fortune in a gold rush, had hidden something valuable in the house! What's more, he'd never returned! They were no longer hunting for a plain ordinary treasure! They were hunting for gold!

"So why are you two so interested in him, anyway?" said Mrs. Turner.

Berry gave a bored sigh. "Oh, we're not interested," she said as she stood up from the table.

"Not interested at all," agreed Terri, standing, too.

They didn't fool anyone. The moment the two girls left the room, everyone hunched forward, whispering. "Andrew Sterling didn't maybe leave a pile of *gold* in all that junk up there?" asked Izzy breathlessly.

Mrs. Turner laughed. "Someone would have found it by now, I'm sure," she said.

"Well, I know they've found something with writing on it, in Spanish," said Melissa. "I translated some of it for them."

48

"And?" said Paul.

"And it didn't make much sense. Anyway they would only let me see a copy."

"Maybe it was written in code," said Tristan, his eyes wide.

"Maybe it was written on a map," said Paul.

Everyone looked at him. "What kind of a map?" said Izzy, hardly daring to imagine.

Paul didn't have to answer. But everybody in the Turner family was smart enough to connect a gold rush with a map and come up with a very exciting thought.

Mr. Turner was the smartest of all. He was able to connect the gold rush and a map to all the dirt in the attic.

"Now don't forget!" he said firmly. "Nobody digs for gold, or anything else in that attic before it's *thoroughly* clean." He sat back, well pleased. Something told Mr. Turner that the attic was going to be spotless before very long.

A little while later, Mrs. Turner stopped by the bedroom door of her youngest daughters. She pretended not to notice as several papers were quickly shoved out of sight.

"Now, I don't want to interrupt your history project, but . . ." she began.

"Oh, you won't do that," said Berry with a small sinking feeling in her stomach. You couldn't interrupt something that wasn't started yet.

"You *could* always write to your great-great-aunt Emily and ask her about Andrew," said Mrs. Turner.

"She's still alive?" said Berry, astonished.

"Very much so," said Mrs. Turner. "Mind you, she's well over ninety. But she's still pretty sharp. She married a rancher. He died years ago, and she lives in Phoenix, Arizona."

"Good, maybe she can give us some clues," said Berry.

"Send her a picture of yourselves," said Mrs. Turner as she left. "Her eyesight is fine. She'll be pleased to know what you look like."

When Mrs. Turner left, Terri got out a pen and a piece of paper. "How much should we tell your great-great-aunt Emily about this?" she said.

"Do you think we should tell her that you were visited by the ghost of her stepbrother?" said Berry.

"I don't think so," said Terri. "Besides, I have

this feeling it was a woman, or a girl. I seem to remember some kind of perfume."

"So? We'll ask her if men wore perfume in 1905," said Berry, grabbing the pen away from Terri. "She's my aunt, so I'll write."

Terri snatched it back. "Are you crazy, Beryllium Turner? If *you* write, she'll be a hundred and eighty by the time she figures out what we're asking."

Chapter Seven

Now they knew a little about Andrew, John, and Emily. But, it wasn't helping them find the treasure.

They had written to Great-Great-Aunt Emily hoping for clues. But they would have to wait for her answer.

Meanwhile, there was only one thing to do—think.

After school the next day they wandered around the house looking for something, anything, that might be made from three yards of pink satin ribbon. Nothing.

They locked themselves in the little sun-room office, and rewrote the clues on the second page of their letter, in case they were written in code.

three yards of pink satin ribbon
ribbon satin pink of yards three
eerht sdray fo knip nitas nobbir
htere aydrs fo ipkn asitn irbbno
t . . . y . . . o . . . p . . . s . . . r, tyopsr, rspoyt

They even translated the clues into Spanish as best they could. Nothing made any sense.

"It's no use," said Terri at last.

"I don't understand," said Berry. "The first page says we won't have any trouble with the instructions. But we're having *terrible* trouble."

Terri was gazing out the window into the backyard. After a moment she said, "What's Tristan doing? He's been out there for ages with Paul's binoculars. Every time I look at him, he seems to be looking right at us."

Berry shrugged. "He said he was bird-watching. Who cares about Tristan? What are we going to do? Give up?"

"Of course not. Forget the instructions. We'll just work with the map. We'll find it, don't worry," said Terri. True Turners never gave up.

But it was Berry who made the big discovery.

Shortly after supper, Terri was drying dishes when she heard a call from upstairs.

"Terri! Up here! I've found something!" It was Berry.

Terri found her stepsister staring out the window of their parents' bedroom. "Look," she

said. "The backyard is the *very* same shape as the map!" said Berry.

Terri looked out the window. *"Our* backyard?" she said doubtfully.

"Of course!" said Berry excitedly. "Turn the map upside down. It's easier that way. See? The missing square is right where our garage is!"

"What about the circle?" Terri asked.

Berry marched Terri out into the garden to show her proof. Terri had seen it before, but had never paid much attention to it.

In the very center of the yard was a low square of paving stones. It stood up an inch or so above the ground and was almost completely overgrown with grass.

These stones were more often heard than seen. First, you heard the angry roar of the lawn mower. Then you heard a loud *braaaattt-clunk* as the lawn mower blade hit the stones and died. After that, nobody was supposed to listen, because either Mr. Turner or Dorothea was using bad language.

"But this is square, not round," said Terri, poking at the stones with her toe.

"But it *is* in the right place," said Berry.

"True."

"And it *might* have had something round sitting on it once."

"We could ask your mom," said Terri.

They found her in the living room. "I don't think I ever knew what they were for," she said, shaking her head. "No, wait. Somehow I can see a birdbath sitting on those stones. Isn't there an old photograph of the garden hanging in the attic?"

A birdbath! Berry and Terri raced to the attic. There *was* an old photo hanging near the door. They dusted it off, held it under the light bulb, and—Eureka!

They rushed back down to their room, punching each other on the shoulder. "Birdbaths are *round!*" said Terri once their door was safely closed.

"And they're full of water. So they can flood!" said Berry. She pointed to the line on the first page of the old letter that talked about an "unfortunate flood."

"We've found it!" cried Terri.

But now they were faced with an enormous problem. How were they going to get permission to dig a big hole in the center of the backyard? What excuse could they possibly give?

*   *   *

Mr. Turner had taken over the backyard as soon as he moved into the house. Now the grass was cut regularly. The hedges were trimmed, too, and a fine flower bed was taking shape along one side.

It made sense to ask Mr. Turner for permission.

They found him in the den watching television with the rest of the family.

"Dad, do you mind if we dig a hole in the backyard?" said Terri.

"Just for fun?" added Berry with a foolish smile.

Mr. Turner looked at her curiously. "Dig a hole for *fun?*"

Terri gave Berry an angry glance. Then she smiled eagerly at her father, trying her best to look as though digging a hole was the most fun thing in the world.

"Where?" he said.

"Oh, anywhere," said Terri, as if it didn't really matter.

Mr. Turner thought for a moment. "Well, as long as it's a *small* hole. There's a bare patch under the trees behind Bart's doghouse. You can't do any harm there."

Terri looked kind of pleased and kind of disappointed. She turned to Berry. Her eyes said, It's your turn, now.

"If it was a really small hole, could we make it by the stones in the middle of the yard?" asked Berry.

"What? Dig a hole in the *grass*? Of course not!" He stared at his two youngest daughters as though they were completely crazy. Everybody else stared, too. They didn't think Berry and Terri were crazy at all.

Berry noticed the stares. "Why don't you all mind your own business. This is a private conversation!" she said angrily.

All the other Turner kids looked away. "Heavens, Berry," said Vanessa. "We couldn't care less about holes you dig in the backyard."

"Yeah!" said Tristan.

"We're not the least bit interested," said Melissa.

"So which side of the stones do you want to dig on?" said Izzy. "Not that I care, of course."

Berry and Terri were too miserable to pay any attention to Izzy. They had failed. The gold would stay hidden under the backyard forever!

Then, just when everything seemed black, Mrs. Turner spoke to her husband. "One thing you might remember, dear. Dorothea's been after you for months to remove those stones," said Mrs. Turner.

"True," agreed Mr. Turner. He thought for a moment.

"If somebody wanted to dig up those stones, I wouldn't have any objection if they carried on and dug a hole there, since there's no grass to ruin."

Berry and Terri looked at each other. Their minds were racing. Once again, their thoughts were exactly the same. True, it wasn't as good as digging *beside* the stones, directly over the X mark.

But if the gold was buried in a trunk, or something, they might see one end of it.

"Thanks! Thanks, Dad!"

The moment they left the room, all their brothers and sisters started whispering to one another.

Chapter Eight

Berry and Terri started their treasure hunt the moment they got home from school the next day.

At first, things went slowly. It took ages to chop away all the thick tufts of grass that had grown over the edges of the stones.

The stones were very heavy. One by one, the girls pried them up and carried them to the back of the garage. At last, they were staring at a bare patch of earth.

"Let's dig," said Terri.

First they tried to dig a very small hole, as close as possible to the X mark on the map. The earth was quite soft and soon the hole grew. The deeper it got, the harder it was to dig without making the hole wider.

As the sun set, the hole grew ever deeper, and ever wider.

Every few shovelfuls, one girl or the other crouched down and examined the side of the hole nearest to the X. Thank goodness, no brothers or sisters seemed to be snooping about.

But they were watching. Behind nearly every window in the house was a pair of greedy eyes.

By the time it was growing dark, there was still no sign of a treasure chest. Did this make the two girls gloomy? Not at all!

With every inch they dug, they knew they were getting closer and closer. Although it was quite dark out in the yard, dirt was flying from the hole faster than ever.

When Mrs. Turner finally came out and forced them to stop, it was too dark even to tell who she was, until she spoke.

Both girls were tired. But they were so excited, they hardly felt any aches or pains from all their digging. "We're only a few inches away! I can feel it!" said Berry as they got ready for bed.

"We'll find it in the morning, for sure!" agreed Terri.

Fortunately for the girls, their bedroom looked out over the front yard. They were able to drop off to sleep quickly, undisturbed by all the strange noises in the backyard that night.

There were scrapes and clanks. There were mutterings. Every now and then, a flashlight clicked on and off.

At the crack of dawn, Berry and Terri were up again. Their muscles were sore, but they didn't care. At breakfast, they were surprised to find they looked fresh compared to some of their brothers and sisters. Paul and Tristan looked especially exhausted.

Out in the backyard, there was another surprise.

Berry was astonished by the size of the dirt pile they had dug up the night before. "Boy! Isn't it weird the way the dark changes things!" said Berry as they stood over the hole.

"What do you mean?" asked Terri.

"Last night, I could have sworn the hole was only about as deep as my knees." She jumped down into it. The sides of the hole came to Berry's waist.

Terri shook her head in amazement. "You're right. We really did dig a lot."

"I just *know* we'll find the treasure before we have to leave for school," said Berry. She began to shovel wildly.

But Berry was wrong.

They didn't find gold after school either, even though they dug the hole right up to their armpits.

Terri's digging began to slow down. At last, she stopped. "I've been thinking," she said.

"Me, too," said Berry.

"We're not really digging in the right place, are we?" said Terri.

"No," agreed Berry.

"The cross is about here, on the grass," said Terri. She leaned out of the hole and drew an imaginary X on the grass. "I was hoping we might see the corner of a box, or a chest or something."

"But we haven't," said Berry.

"So what are we going to do about it?" said Terri.

"I think we have to dig where the X is marked," said Berry.

Terri shook her head. "Dad said we couldn't dig on the grass."

"We won't," said Berry. "I have an idea."

After supper Berry got down into their hole with a garden trowel and showed Terri her idea.

"The grass is like a carpet, see?" said Berry. She began to dig earth away underneath the grass in the direction of the imaginary X. "I can tunnel right under it, and it will stay in one piece."

Terri liked the idea. "Don't dig too close to it, though," she warned. But Berry was determined to miss nothing. Soon she was scrabbling like a dog, her head and shoulders hidden under the grass.

Normally *Terri* was the hardest worker. But this wasn't her favorite kind of job. It was far too messy. As the tunnel under the grass grew larger and deeper, Berry began to look like a living, wriggling lump of dirt.

So Terri stood behind Berry in the hole. Now and then, she shoveled up dirt that was falling around her feet and threw it on the pile beside the hole.

"We can't possibly miss it now," said Berry. Her voice was muffled.

"I hope so," said Terri, looking up anxiously. She had just felt a drop of rain.

Dusk fell. It was made even gloomier by the heavy clouds overhead. Soon rain was coming down quite heavily.

Still the tunnel under the grass grew. Berry was lying on her stomach now, only her legs visible. Gold fever had made her tireless.

Terri excused herself for a moment. She returned with an umbrella. The rain was turning the dirt in the bottom of the hole to mud.

For a while, things were all right for Berry inside her cozy tunnel. The grass kept the rain off. Berry was filthy, but not wet.

But in the end, water did begin leaking through the carpet above her head. The dirt on Berry turned slowly into muck. The water trickled around her into the dirt underneath. She began to feel as if she was lying in a tub of pudding.

"This is fun!" called Berry, her voice muffled.

Terri shook her head in disbelief. "Don't make the hole any wider!" she shouted. "The grass is beginning to sag over your head." Terri didn't think it was fun. Standing out in the rain, it was wet and cold. Terri was beginning to feel tired, too.

And the more tired she became, the more she began to worry. Suppose, just suppose, that Andrew Sterling had accidentally marked the X on the wrong side of the hole? What a disaster that would be!

Terri turned and studied the mud wall behind her. Then she called her stepsister. Berry slipped out of her mud slide and stood in the rain, looking at the other side of the hole, too.

"How could he be *that* careless?" said Berry.

"He was a Sterling, remember?" said Terri.

"You mean, somebody who wasn't afraid to get

dirty if they had to," said Berry angrily. She flicked some of the mud off her shirt onto Terri.

"What's that supposed to mean?" said Terri, kicking gloop from the bottom of the hole over Berry's shins.

"Well, you started it," said Berry, wiping her muddy sleeve against Terri's clean one.

Then, just in time to prevent a fight, another voice cried out in the backyard. "Great Scott!" It was Mr. Turner.

The two girls wheeled around. He was striding across the backyard toward them. Mr. Turner was dapper as always, with a neat blue raincoat over the blazer and gray flannels he wore to work.

There was a look of horror on his face. "Are you digging to China? What on earth is that enormous pile of dirt doing there? Don't you realize it will kill the grass?"

"Dad, don't—"

"I thought you were digging for fun, not building a subway!"

"Dad, stop—" Mr. Turner wasn't listening. He was walking straight toward the sagging patch of grass!

"I want you two girls to stop this nonsense right

66

now, and *whoaaoh!"* Berry and Terri had designed the perfect dad-trap.

Mr. Turner's feet piunged through the carpet of grass sod. They struck the slippery chute and the lawn swallowed up Mr. Turner.

A split second later he slurped out of Berry's side tunnel, and into the mud at the bottom of the main hole. His legs tangled with Berry and Terri and they tumbled over on top of him.

By the time all three were standing again, they were covered head to toe in mud.

Mr. Turner's anger was awesome. It was not made any better by Mrs. Turner and Dorothea. They came out of the house and laughed and laughed. "The three little pigs," said Mrs. Turner as she drenched the three, one after another, with the garden hose.

"My clothes are ruined!" roared Mr. Turner.

"Nonsense!" said Mrs. Turner. "They'll clean up just fine."

Finally, even Mr. Turner started to chuckle. Then everybody was laughing.

"But none of this will be so funny if you girls kill all the grass," said Mr. Turner at last.

"No, sir," they both mumbled.

"I want that hole filled tonight," said Mr. Turner. "I don't care how long it takes!"

Poor Berry and Terri. They had felt no aches and pains while they were digging for gold. Now, they could hardly lift their arms. The dirt pile was heavy with water. Every shovelful weighed a ton. It grew darker and darker.

At last, Mr. Turner took pity on them. Dressed in jeans and an old jacket, he arrived at the hole. He took one look at the pale, rain-streaked faces of his two youngest children and softened. He kissed each one on the ear.

"Go to bed, you idiots," he said. "Tomorrow, do that history project you keep putting off. No digging, understand?" Then he picked up a shovel and started to work.

Chapter Nine

It was Saturday morning. Berry awoke to find Terri with her covers up to her chin. She was staring wide-eyed at Berry.

"What's wrong?" said Berry.

"Am I awake?" said Terri anxiously.

Berry pinched herself. "Ow! I don't know about you, but I am," she said.

"Berry, I saw the ghost again!" said Terri breathlessly. "I don't know if it was a dream, or what."

"No! What did it do?" said Berry, sitting on Terri's bed.

"It walked across the room again, only toward your bed. I thought it was going to whisper in your ear," said Terri.

Berry shook her head. "If it did, I didn't hear anything," she said. "Darn!"

"Then maybe it wrote something else on the map. I saw it look in your sock drawer where you keep it."

Berry quickly checked the map. But there were no marks on it, nor on the two pages of the letter.

"Was it a man, or a woman?" said Berry.

"It was so dark," said Terri. "But I *think* it was a woman, or a girl," she said. "Anyway, it was probably only a dream."

After breakfast, Berry and Terri dragged their aching bodies into the sun-room and looked out into the backyard. The pile of dirt was gone, along with the hole.

"If the treasure *was* buried there, it'll be buried forever," said Berry gloomily.

"I hate to say it, Beryllium," said Terri. "But I really think we'd better do this dumb history thing. We've only got today and tomorrow, you know."

Berry was too tired to argue. So they cleared off the top of the little desk. Then they arranged their history textbooks beside clean sheets of paper.

There could be no more excuses. It was the last possible moment to start their history project. They sat down to think.

Terri had the first important idea.

"Why would anybody draw those extra straight lines on a map, unless they were being really careful? I mean, gardens don't need super-straight lines."

Berry shrugged.

"I think it has to be a map of a building, or a room," said Terri.

"Wait," said Berry. She closed her eyes. "There *are* two rooms in the house that have that shape—the living room and the den." So they went to look.

Berry was not quite correct, though. The shape of the den wasn't right. The bite was missing from the wrong corner of it.

Only the living room was exactly the right shape. "Except, where's the circle?" said Berry, waving to the center of the floor. Instead of a circle, there were large pink and red flowers scattered all over the living-room rug.

"What about under the rug?" Terri said.

Berry guarded the door. Terri quickly moved the coffee table and rolled back the carpet. There was a great deal of dust, but no circle.

"This rug hasn't been here since 1905, though," said Terri.

"You know, there *is* a really big old rug rolled up out in the garage," Berry said.

"Maybe we should peek at it just before we start our history project," said Terri.

The rug was far too heavy for the two of them to move. Luckily, Paul happened to be passing the open garage door. He was strangely helpful. He went and found Tristan. The two boys dragged the rug around into the backyard.

Berry and Terri trailed behind, explaining. "We thought we'd spread it out in the sun and do our homework on it," said Berry.

"I'll bet you did," said Paul, and he winked at Tristan.

All four of them unrolled the rug. All four of them stared at the faded design. There was a wide, square border, and all kinds of fancy curlicues scattered over it. Right in the center was a large circle!

That afternoon, many eyes watched Berry and Terri from the house. Berry and Terri did not even pretend to do schoolwork. They found a measuring tape, and they measured.

"It *must* have been a living-room rug," said Berry a little later as they finished measuring the living room. "It's the only room in the house big enough for it."

"This is it! This is it! At last!" said Terri, bouncing up and down with excitement. The excitement didn't last.

Here in the living room, Terri was bouncing above floorboards, not dirt. How could they dig?

"It *has* to be hidden under the floorboards," said Berry. Could they be lifted? At the edge of the room Berry poked at a loose floorboard. The nails were loose. "Terri, maybe we could—"

"No, we couldn't," said Terri firmly. "Not after last night."

Berry knew that Terri was right. They were so close to the treasure, they could practically touch it. But there was nothing they could do about it. How frustrating!

"I suppose we'd better go do our history project," said Terri with a sigh. They went back outside and sat on the rug.

They couldn't concentrate.

Berry lay on her back and pretended she was flying on a magic carpet to Paris, France. A trunk full of gold rode along at her side.

Terri sat and numbered a whole lot of lines in a notebook. She reached number 242. She still couldn't think of one idea for their history project.

Later that afternoon, their father rescued them. He invited the whole family down to his cinema for a free movie. Berry and Terri were glad to escape for a while. All through the house, they could feel the heat of the gold beating up through the floorboards.

Chapter Ten

On Sunday morning, everyone woke very late—and very grumpy. It was a long time before the bathroom was clear. Berry slipped inside, closed the door, pulled the shower curtain, and began to run a nice private bath.

And so, thanks to Berry and her bath, Terri found where the treasure was hidden.

Mr. Turner and Terri were both in the den. Terri was lying on the couch, half asleep. Her father was sipping coffee and staring at the TV, which was not turned on.

Suddenly Mr. Turner jumped as if he had been stung. He looked at the back of his hand. There was a drop of water on it. He looked up at the ceiling and shouted, "Berry! Have you got the shower curtain in the bathtub?"

Terri, lying beside her father, had to hide a smile with her hand. Mr. Turner had insisted that his own children should not pick up bad habits from the sloppy Sterling family. But here he was, bellowing at the ceiling just like they did.

She looked up and watched another drop fall from the plaster. Terri knew what was happening. Berry wasn't having a shower, she was having a bath. She usually filled it so full that water slopped over the side whenever she moved. The whole floor was often flooded.

Upstairs there was a faint cry from Berry. "Sorry!" she said. Terri's eye now wandered along the crack in the ceiling where the water was leaking. It was very straight.

Indeed, now that she looked, there was a pattern of faint cracks on the ceiling, all straight.

"What makes those?" she asked, pointing out the cracks to her father.

"Those? Oh, they've just formed over the years," said Mr. Turner. "They're made by the beams that hold up the floor upstairs. They run right across the house."

And suddenly, lying there looking, Terri saw the treasure map. The shape of the ceiling was right. The faint lines on the ceiling matched the lines ruled across the map.

And there, set in the ceiling, was a painted circle. It was the base of an old chandelier, long since removed.

Another drip from the ceiling caught her eye,

and she knew what the letter meant by "the unfortunate flood." It had been a flood in the bathroom.

Terri found where the treasure was buried, not by looking down, but by looking up.

She slipped quietly out of the room. A moment later she was beating on the bathroom door. "I've found it for sure this time," she called, her voice quivering with excitement.

Several minutes later Mr. Turner, still half asleep, took another sip of coffee and was surprised to see Berry lying on the couch, instead of Terri. He blinked and shook his head. Surely he was not beginning to confuse his daughter with his stepdaughter.

He looked again a moment later, and there was *nobody* on the couch. Berry and Terri were whispering excitedly in the hall.

"What do we do?" said Terri.

"I think there's only one thing we *can* do," said Berry.

"Tell my dad?" said Terri. Berry nodded.

It was the right decision. At first he was too sleepy to pay attention. Then he was too interested in the letter, the map, and finally the ceiling over his head.

"This is *exciting!*" Mr. Turner said at last. "It looks like you may have found it, whatever it is."

Mr. Turner brought a stepladder and a screwdriver from the basement. He propped the ladder under the base of the chandelier. Berry and Terri steadied the ladder while Mr. Turner attacked the ceiling.

"Well, at least we don't have to dig to China," he said as he found, one by one under the paint, the screws that held the base to the ceiling.

Gently, Mr. Turner pried away the round metal plate. Dirt and dust showered down around his shoulders. The girls clustered around, gawking upward. They turned away, blinking, their eyes full of dirt.

When they looked back, they saw . . . nothing but a hole. But at the edge of the hole, clearly in view, was one of the floorbeams marked on the map.

"On that side, Dad. Look on that side," said Terri.

"I can't look," said her father. "The ladder isn't high enough." Instead, he reached carefully into the ceiling.

"Ah!" he said.

"What? What?" said Berry and Terri.

"It's not a treasure chest, that's for sure," said Mr. Turner. He was tugging something toward him. "It feels like some kind of bundle."

And that's what he handed down to the two girls. It was a narrow, floppy white bundle about two feet long, bound up with a faded pink ribbon.

"The satin ribbon!" cried Berry and Terri at once.

"I'm afraid it's not heavy enough for gold," said Mr. Turner as he climbed down.

All three of them stood staring at the bundle as it lay on the coffee table.

"Are you going to open it, Dad?" said Terri.

"Of course not," Mr. Turner said. "You've certainly earned the right to do it, both of you."

"Do you suppose we should call everybody else?" said Berry. Now that they had found the bundle there seemed no point in keeping a secret.

"Sure," Terri said. And so they did.

"Oh!" squeaked Terri as Berry unwrapped a corner of the old sheet that wrapped the bundle. A pale, white face was staring out at them.

"It's only a doll, silly," said Berry. But what a doll! It was a gorgeous, old-fashioned china doll with black hair and a red velvet dress.

The doll was passed from hand to hand. Every single girl in the Turner house said, "I want it!"

One by one, a strange and beautiful collection of old things came out of the bundle. There was a heavy silver-backed brush and comb. There was a tiny doll made of cornstalks. A worn purse covered in faded beads held several silver hairpins and a heavy gold bracelet.

A locket held a miniature painting of a woman. "I believe that's your great-great-grandmother, Martha Sterling," said Mrs. Turner, studying the face.

There were several more fascinating things in the bundle, including a pair of black patent leather shoes and a sealed envelope.

The family passed it from hand to hand. On the front, written in familiar neat handwriting, were the words, "My Most Valuable Possessions."

Terri slit the letter open. Inside were two pages. The first page was a list of most of the things they had taken from the bundle. The last words on the page were, "My best bracelet made of real . . ."

Terri turned the page to read the rest of the sentence. But the second page was unreadable. It was the now-familiar code.

"That's Spanish, and backward," said Berry. So

Vanessa quickly translated each word. Terri wrote the words down, then reversed them. Everyone leaned over her shoulder to read.

I hid the bundle in the ceiling in the small parlor. You will probably have to take down the chandelier to get it. It was easy to hide, because all the plaster had fallen off the ceiling in the unfortunate flood.

If you find this letter and I am still alive, please put it back. If I never come back, my sister Emily can have everything. She is a nuisance, but I love her all the same.

"How remarkable!" said Mr. Turner.

"Why would Andrew Sterling call a bunch of girl's things, 'my most valuable possessions'?" said Terri.

"Who knows?" said Mrs. Turner with a shrug. "But one thing is for sure. He was obviously a true sloppy Sterling."

"Why?" said Berry.

"Because he mixed up the letters, didn't he?" she said, holding up the first page of the list. "My best bracelet made of real . . . what? Why gold, of course." Mrs. Turner showed them the top word on the page found in the attic.

"So the gold and the pink satin ribbon and stuff were part of Andrew's list!" exclaimed Berry.

"And the second page of the instructions got put in the ceiling by mistake!" said Terri.

"Just the kind of thing *you'd* do, Berry," said Mrs. Turner, turning to her youngest daughter. "Hey, why are you suddenly so glum?"

"We can't keep any of it," said Berry. "The letter says it should go to Great-Aunt Emily."

"Good point, Berry," said Mr. Turner approvingly.

"Still, I bet she'd be excited, too," said Berry, brightening. "Could we call her and tell her?"

"I don't see why not," said their mother. "I talk to her every Christmas on the phone. After dinner, okay?"

They didn't need to call, though. Great-Aunt Emily called them first.

The call came at supper. Mrs. Turner answered the kitchen phone. A moment later she poked her head into the dining room. "It's your great-aunt Emily," she whispered, her hand over the phone.

"She sounds very excited. She wants to talk to Berry and Terri."

Mrs. Turner sent Berry to the extension in her bedroom, and Terri to the one in the office. "I'll just listen," she promised, still holding the kitchen phone.

"Berry? Terri? It was wonderful to hear from you!" The voice at the other end of the line was strong and clear. "Which one of you is the blond one?"

"Me! Berry."

"My lord, how you took me back, Berry. You're the spitting image of my older sister, Anne."

Immediately there was a spluttering on the line. It was Mrs. Turner. "Aunt Emily! I didn't know you had an older sister!"

"Ssh!" said Berry crossly. "You promised you wouldn't speak, Mom."

"And you found a letter from her, too, I understand?" said Great-Aunt Emily. "It couldn't be Andrew, you know. He was long gone by 1905."

"More than that, Aunt Emily," said Berry. "We found all kinds of things that must have belonged to her."

There was a gasp at the other end of the line.

"Not—not the doll with the red velvet dress!" said Great-Aunt Emily.

"Yup," said Berry.

"Oh, my! Oh, my! I so wanted to get my hands on that doll. We knew she'd hidden it, John and I. We looked everywhere, but—"

Mrs. Turner could stand it no longer. She interrupted again. "But, Aunt Emily! How is it that I've never heard of Anne?"

There was a silence at the other end of the phone. Finally, Great-Aunt Emily spoke. There was a slight quaver in her voice now. "It was terribly sad, my dear," she said. "After it happened, nobody talked about her much anymore."

All at once, Berry and Terri had the same feeling. Neither of them wanted to listen anymore. But neither of them could tear themselves away from the phone.

"Anne was my father's favorite," said Great-Aunt Emily. "She had the best of everything. The best clothes, and the best toys. How John and I envied her!

"My father wanted her to have the best schooling, too. So when she was twelve—that was in 1905—he decided to send her to San Francisco to live with our aunt and attend a better school than was available in San Diego.

"She didn't want to go. She felt something terrible was going to happen to her. Indeed, one day she deliberately flooded the upstairs bathroom, trying to make my father mad at her. It brought down all the plaster in the ceiling of the small parlor. You've never seen such a mess!

"It was no use. My father sent her anyway," said Great-Aunt Emily. Then she paused for a long time.

"What happened?" said Berry at last.

"The next spring there was the great earthquake in San Francisco. She and our aunt died in the fire that followed the earthquake. Oh, I loved her so much!" said Great-Aunt Emily. Then she started to cry.

That's when Berry started to cry, too. Then Terri. The phone call was more or less over.

There were lots of wet eyes in the rest of the family. Mrs. Turner gathered everybody around the little bundle of belongings in the den and explained just what it meant.

Of the two girls, Terri recovered first. Anne Sterling was not, after all, her relation. But Berry was heartbroken. The entire family wound up sitting on her bed, trying to make her feel better.

"But I feel like *I* died," blubbered Berry. "She looked like me. She was sloppy like me. She was the favorite kid in the family like me." At this last remark, everybody looked at one another over Berry's head and crossed their eyes.

"Berry, she wasn't exactly like you," said her mother gently. "Look at her handwriting, for a start."

"I guess," said Berry, between sobs.

"And she wouldn't be alive now, anyhow," said Mr. Turner.

"But it's so *sad!*" wailed Berry.

Finally, Berry cried herself out. She lay in bed and listened to the faint sounds of the rest of the family, who were downstairs, marveling over the old belongings of Anne Sterling.

At last, Berry could stand it no longer. She went down and joined them. By bedtime, both she and Terri were cheerful enough for Mr. Turner to make a point.

"You've had quite a little adventure, girls," he said. "But there's a price to pay. Tomorrow afternoon, what are you going to hand in for a history project? You've made your bed. Now you'll truly have to lie in it."

But, for once, Mr. Turner was wrong. At lunchtime the next day, Berry and Terri went to the library and made some photocopies of old newspaper headlines about the Great San Francisco Earthquake and Fire.

Then they took the photocopies and Anne Sterling's belongings to school for everyone to see.

"My Most Precious Possessions, the best-loved things of a little girl who died in the Great Earthquake and Fire of 1906" was the title of their history project. They each got A pluses. Terri decided that she loved history after all.

Chapter Eleven

Great-Aunt Emily didn't want the doll after all. "Well, of course I do, my dears," she explained on the phone to Berry and Terri. "But not as much as I did in 1905. And not as much as you two want her, today."

"Oh, no. We don't want her," said Berry, lying bravely.

"Nobody wants her. She's yours," agreed Terri on the extension phone.

"Well, I don't know what to say, I'm so disappointed," said Great-Aunt Emily. "It's only my second phone call with two very attractive young grand-nieces. And they think so little of me that they're telling me lies! Goodness, I might cry again."

"Please don't do that, Aunt Emily," pleaded Berry. "We do want the doll a bit."

"A lot, really," said Terri.

"More than anything else in the world," admitted Berry.

"Well, now. That's better!" said Great-Aunt

Emily. "Her name is Abigail and you may both have her, on one condition."

"Yes?" said Berry and Terri eagerly.

"You must bring her to visit me in Phoenix, Arizona. You'll have to talk your mother and father into it, promise?"

Berry and Terri promised.

"We'd be delighted, Aunt Emily," added Mrs. Turner, who was listening on the kitchen extension.

"And I must have one more promise from young Berry," said Great-Aunt Emily.

"Me?" said Berry.

"You do look most terribly like my dear sister, Anne. I will probably cry again when we first meet, my dear," said Great-Aunt Emily. "You must promise to be brave and not cry yourself."

"I promise," said Berry solemnly. But already her lower lip was quivering again. It was not a promise that Berry Turner expected to keep.

Ma chère Annamarie,

Spooky happenings in the Turner house! Terri got visited by two ghosts!

The second was a fake. Izzy told us that it

was her, taking a peek at the treasure map we found.

But who was the first ghost? The one that told her how to find the attic? Mom and Vanessa, and Izzy and Melissa and Dorothea all swear it wasn't them.

Terri is sure it was Anne Sterling, come to find her favorite things. Terri wants to sleep with the lights on every night now. What a bore! If it is Anne Sterling, I want to see her! She's supposed to look just like you!

> Your long-lost twin and step-triplet,
> Beryllium

High under the peak of the roof at the back of the Turner House, there was a vent that allowed cool air to blow through the attic. Once there had been a letter hidden up in the vent. Now it was gone.

But on sunny afternoons, when the light was just right, it was possible to see a pale patch behind the vent. It looked like a ghostly white face, trapped forever high in the rafters.

Berry and Terri played in the backyard, but

they never looked up and saw it. They were always too busy arguing. Not about which girl knew the most about their house, though. Berry didn't lose too many arguments. But she had lost that one.